The Stones
And the Poet

A story based on *Two Stones*
a poem written in 826 by Bai Juyi

Lynn Connor
Illustrated by Lu Kesi

Lan Su Chinese Garden
Portland, Oregon

For my granddaughters
Emily, Layla, and Yasmeen

– L.C.

*"Stones of amazing shapes
embody the wonders of all times."*

– Luo Ye

沁
香
仙
館
石

The Stones

Year after year the water of Lake Tai washed over the grey green stones. The water wore holes in the stones. The surfaces of the stones were wrinkly like an old grandfather's face. The stones twisted and turned in strange, irregular shapes. Some were taller than a man; some were not so tall.

What could anyone do with these strange stones? They could not be used for roads or walk ways or to build walls. What use is a wall, a walk way or a road with holes in it? The stones were useless for anything practical, so no one ever bothered with them.

For hundreds of years after hundreds of years, the stones were ignored and the water of Lake Tai continued to shape them. Mud caked on them and moss grew in the cracks and crevices. Useless, ugly stones.

白居易

The Poet

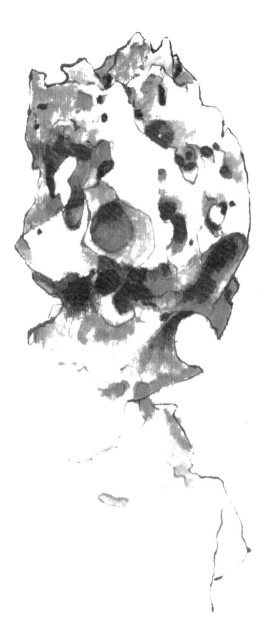

太湖石

In the year 825 the Emperor of China appointed Bai Juyi governor of Suzhou near Lake Tai. It was an important government position. Yet, he was reluctant to go to Suzhou. He wanted to work in his garden, visit with his friends, and write poetry.

Centuries old Suzhou was a large, busy and beautiful city. It was famous as a gathering spot for scholars and for its beautiful women. Like all Chinese cities it was surrounded by a wall. This wall was ten miles long and had eight land gates and eight water gates. Inside the wall roads and canals crisscrossed the city. Markets, temples, military barracks, granaries, storehouses, inns, homes, and gardens filled the city. In the middle of the city was a walled "small city" with government offices. This is where Bai Juyi worked and lived.

賞
勝

Outside the city wall, boats traveled up and down the Grand Canal carrying rice, salt, copper, and travelers. To the west improbable-looking hills rose sharply from the low lands making them look like mountains. Beyond them was Lake Tai. To the east were scattered small lakes. Rivers and streams wandered between the hills and the lakes. Farm villages dotted the countryside. All of this, inside the wall and outside the wall, was Bai Juyi's responsibility.

The work of the city and countryside kept Bai Juyi busy from morning to night, day after day, month after month. He wrote to friends, "I spend the morning going through government papers, I spend the evening going through government papers. There are still many at which I have not looked, and already the crickets are chirping close to my seat."

錦雲堂石

He further complained, "At dawn I confront a pile of papers, dusk comes before I can get away. The beauty of the morning, the beauty of the afternoon pass while I sit clamped to an office desk."

When Bai Juyi was not doing paper work, he inspected the roads, waterways, farms, and markets. He was always busy. He did not have time for friends and poetry. He was tired and often sick from all of the work. Bai Juyi was lonely.

浣花春雨

Three Friends

One day when inspecting the area along the shore of Lake Tai, Bai Juyi saw the dirty, misshapen stones. The stones intrigued him. Pole bearers carried two large stones back to his office.

Bai Juyi scrubbed away the dirt and mud to find dark hollows, crevices green with moss, and shapes that looked like coiled old dragons. These stones were so different from any others, Bai Juyi wondered if they fell from the sky.

He walked around each stone looking and looking at the strange and wonderful shape of each. One stone towered like a steep mountain, a perfect place to lean his zither.

太湖石

The other stone had a hollow just right to place his wine cup.

Bai Juyi smiled and thought, "Every person has something he loves, and all things yearn to have a companion." Then Bai Juyi turned his head and asked the pair of stones if they would keep an old man company. Although the stones were powerless to speak, they agreed the three should be friends.

Bai Juyi returned to his paper work, no longer lonely—on his left his zither leaned on one stone and on his right the other stone held his wine cup.

倒影清漪

The Poem

沁香仙館石

Bai Juyi told the story of his stones in a poem, "Two Stones." Many years after he left Suzhou and lived hundreds of miles away, he still thought about the strange and wonderful stones from Lake Tai. Bai Juyi wondered if "a hundred years, a thousand years from now the stones might be scattered, mysteriously appearing all around the world. Who knows where they will go?"

Many people read Bai Juyi's poem. They wanted the stones, too. Even Chinese emperors wanted the stones for their gardens. People visiting China saw the strange stones from Lake Tai. They, too, wanted the stones. The stones were no longer useless and ugly. The gnarled stones of Lake Tai are now in gardens all around the world.

蒼然兩片石厥狀怪且醜俗用無所堪時人嫌

不取叶韻結從胚渾始得自洞庭口萬古遺水

濱一朝入吾手擔舁來郡內洗刷去泥垢孔黑

煙痕深罅青苔色厚老蛟蟠作足古劍插為首

忽疑天上落不似人間有一可支吾琴一可貯

吾酒峭絕高數尺坳泓容一斗五絃倚其左一

盃置其右窪樽酌未空玉山頹已久人皆有所

好物各求其偶漸恐少年場不容垂白叟迴頭

問雙石能伴老夫否石雖不能言許我為三友

Two grey green chunks of stone,
their shapes are strange and ugly.
They have no practical use,
people dislike them and do not take them.
Formed in ancient chaos,
they took shape in Lake Tai.
Ten thousand years abandoned at the water's edge,
then one morning they came into my hands.
Pole-bearers brought them to my office,
I washed and scrubbed away mud and stains.
Holes with deep dark misty scars,
crevices with thick lichen colored mosses.
Like old dragons coiled to form the feet,
and antique swords stuck in for the head.
I wondered if they fell from the sky,
so unlike anything in this world.
One perfect for leaning my zither,
one perfect for holding my wine.
One like a very steep hill, several feet tall,
the other with a hollow like a deep pool.
My five-string zither leans on the left one,
my wine cup is placed on the right one.
People all have things they love,
and things all yearn for a companion.
More and more I fear young people
will not welcome a white-haired old man.
Turning my head I ask the two stones,
"Will you keep an old man company?"
The stones even though they can not speak
Promise we will be three friends.

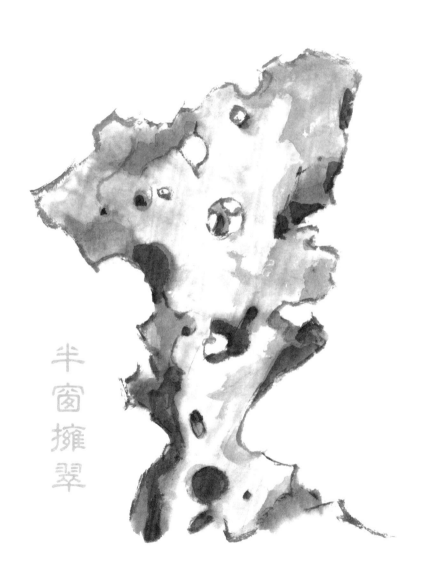

半窗擁翠

Author's Note

Edward H. Schafer in *Tu Wan's Stone Catalogue of Cloudy Forest: A Commentary and Synopsis* states that Du Wan's twelfth century book attributes the fame of the stones to Bai Juyi.

The basis of the story in this book is Bai Juyi's poem "Two Stones" (Shuang Shi). It is supplemented by Bai Juyi's "Essay on Lake Tai Stones" (Tai Hu Shi Ji), information in Fan Chengda's *Annals of Suzhou* (Wu Jun Zhi) written in the late 12th century which includes a section on the Lake Tai stones under "Commodities" and Arthur Waley's *The Life and Times of Po Chu-I [Bai Juyi]*, 772-846 which includes excerpts of Bai Juyi's letters to friends when he was governor of Suzhou.

— Lynn Connor

另一塊石頭

Illustrator's Note

Each of the stones you see illustrated in this book can be found (though some may be hiding) in the Lan Su Chinese Garden in Portland, Oregon (USA). For more information about the Garden visit their website at www.lansugarden.org.

The Chinese say that when you drink water you must think about its source. So I mustn't forget to thank my teacher — thank you Wang Gongyi.

— Lu Kesi

石
韻

Copyright ©2010 by Lan Su Chinese Garden
Text and translation copyright ©2006 by
Lynn Connor
Designed and illustrated by Lu Kesi
Printed at Ash Creek Press
ISBN 978-0-615-34970-1

Lan Su Chinese Garden
P.O. Box 3706
Portland, Oregon 97208
503.228.8131
www.lansugarden.org

Publisher's Cataloging-in-Publication

Connor, Lynn.
    The stones and the poet : a story based on Two
Stones, a poem written in 826 by Bai Juyi / Lynn
Connor; illustrated by Lu Kesi.
    p. cm.
    SUMMARY: The poet Bai Juyi (772-846) brings fame
to the strange, useless stones of Lake Tai, China.
    Audience: Grades K-5.
    ISBN-13: 978-0-615-34970-1
    ISBN-10: 0-615-34970-6

    1. Bai, Juyi, 772-846. Shuang shi--Juvenile
literature. 2. Rocks--China--Tai Lake--History--
Juvenile literature. 3. Tai Lake (China)--History--
Juvenile fiction. [1. Bai, Juyi, 772-846. Shuang shi.
2. Rocks--History. 3. Tai Lake (China)--History.]
I. Bai, Juyi, 772-846. Shuang shi. English. II. Lu, Kesi,
ill. III. Title.

    PL2674.A75C66 2010   895.1'13
                    QBI10-600023

Draw a stone – a real one or an imaginary one. Give your stone a name. The stone on the cover of this book is called "Crescent Cloud."

Write a poem or story about a stone.